WILD BLUEBERRIES
FIVE LOVE STORIES

MAUREEN MCNEAL

EMPEROR BOOKS

Wild Blueberries

Copyright © 2022 by Maureen McNeal

All rights reserved.

Published by Emperor Books

Bellerose Village, New York

ISBN

Print 978-1-63777-343-7

Digital 978-1-63777-342-0

Final photo credit – Wild Blueberries

Photograph cover credit: Janet Neuhauser

Janet.neuhauser@gmail.com

This pinhole photograph "Eclipse, Top of the World" was a 20 minute film exposure made during the 2017 North American solar eclipse in Washington State.

For Martha

WILD BLUEBERRIES

VERED'S MOTHER Kitty painted landscapes en plein air; her father Sammy was a night watchman at the Bremerton Navy Yard. On Sundays, Sammy drove the family to a wild blueberry field near Crescent Lake on the Olympic Peninsula so Kitty could paint. Her long hair pinned beneath a straw hat, she tied a smock over her torso and set up her easel. Vered and her little brother, Arno, played catch with a red ball until Arno tired, and laid down to nap on the picnic blanket next to his snoring father. Vered practiced her ballet positions barefoot among the wild blueberries. She wanted to be an artist like her mother.

"I'm hungry," Arno whined.

Kitty walked the children through the woods while Sammy set out the picnic lunch of ham sandwiches, pickles, pie with buttery crust and lemonade. He sang a German opera to scare the black bear away while he picked the tiny berries. The children ate more sweet morsels than they put into the cans on strings around their necks. Arno went off to play with his truck while Vered held his red ball in one arm. On tip-toe, she practiced a pirouette. Knees bent, she jumped onto her toes, her heels lifting off the ground. The red ball soared over the field toward a brilliant golden orb on the horizon. Spinning faster and faster toward the light, she lost track of the picnic blanket. Two small people with large heads, no taller than her mother, stood in front of a spaceship.

"Vered!" her father called. He grabbed her and ran back for Kitty. Still absorbed in her painting, Kitty's smock caught on the easel. She tripped and rolled toward the spaceship. A door opened and the two small people retreated. The family shielded their faces as the bright ship rocketed in the shape of a triangle, straight up into the sky. Vered waved good-bye.

"Get in the car," Sammy said to Vered. He dragged mother and daughter over and opened the door. Arno was already in the backseat, his mouth and hands splayed on the window. Sammy jammed the car into gear and rocked back onto the highway.

"You scared them, Daddy," Vered cried, her face furious. He didn't understand that dancing in the light of the spaceship was the happiest moment of her life.

"Don't you ever tell anyone what you saw, do you hear me, Vered? Never, never, never mention this to anyone."

While Sammy was at work the next day, Kitty and Vered drove back to Crescent Lake. Kitty never drove anywhere except to town and the wheels of the car tapped the road like a blind man's stick with her oversteering. Animals in the night had finished the ham sandwiches but the half pie was undisturbed in its carrier. Kitty found her straw hat, smock and easel. She touched up the oil painting while Vered searched the blueberry patch for Arno's red ball. The spaceship might land again, Vered thought, if she could only dance. Instead, thunder rumbled between the mountain peaks. The faster the windshield wipers swished, the slower Kitty drove home. Vered studied her mother's oil painting on the back seat: she had not painted Vera and her brother in the wild blueberries but the two small people standing in front of their spaceship, lit like a yellow bonfire.

"You are my rose," Vered's mother told her before she died.

Vered was in high school, and her father remarried soon after. His new wife loved Arno but not Vered. Desperately, she tried to win the new mother with her dances, but her father disowned her.

Without college tuition, Vered moved to Seattle, got a night job at Boeing and took dance classes at University of Washington. She was invited to joined Eleanor King's dance company and it was Eleanor's positive attitude that helped Vered survive the loss of her mother and the crippling experience of her father's abandonment. For the first time, Vered expressed a tenderness toward her own body as she danced the choreographic work of Doris Humphry—*Life of the Bees, Shakers,* and *Water Study.* Doris Humphrey was the great grandmother of modern dance.

"You must study in New York City," Eleanor King said.

Vered bought a one-way bus ticket and in the bottom of her suitcase, packed the painting her mother had hidden away. In Manhattan, she took at room at Spellman Hall, a YWCA women's residence in Abingdon Square in the West Village. Propped on the windowsill of her room, she noticed for the first time Arno's red ball floating between the two small people. New York City hummed with energy, but each afternoon before teaching children ballet at the Midtown Manhattan "Y", it was her mother's landscape she studied: the red ball levitated inside her; the spaceship charged her with a gravitational pull toward the future.

Auditioning at the Martha Graham School of Dance, Vered took her turn on the floor. Martha, the mother of modern dance, unclasped the thin gold necklace around Vered's neck, and said: "You are a sensitive young woman, Vered. The human form is naturally beautiful. I want you to envision a red ball. Now lift, spin and soar across the room."

A STRANGE BREATHLESS STUNT

SHE WOKE stiff and bruised in the hip after sleeping the night on a bench at the Artichoke Restaurant. It was awkward waking in such a public place. Peering out of the musty sleeping bag, she watched gulls circle the orange tin roof building across the street and the occasional car slowing in the grey dawn toward the stop light in downtown Olympia. A familiar cold, musty, wood stove-smell caused her to bolt upright. LB—one of her five male restaurant partners and an ex-boyfriend—grinned over her.

"Good! You're awake," he said.

"How long have you been standing there?" she asked.

He retreated to the old-fashioned glassed-in office left over from the meat market days and set a record on the stereo. *Sugar Magnolia* blasted the dining room. She should have remembered that LB baked bread three mornings a week, thirty-six loaves in total. She cringed to think of him creeping around while she slept among the upside down chairs on top of twenty unmatched wooden tables. She pulled on yesterday's army pants and wool socks, slipped into her wooden clogs and buttoned her cranberry sweater over her t-shirt. She entered the tiny bathroom and locked the door.

The old clock in the office said five-forty-five—too early to call Clare who always managed to make Bemy laugh when things went wrong. Clare was short in stature, freckled, well-read, and when she got excited her thick wavy hair rocked like choppy water. They met in line getting their Evergreen State College Photo ID taken. Clare was looking for a roommate to split the fifty-five dollar a month rent in a downtown apartment. Bemy didn't like Clare's long-haired cat but after a bowl of home-made vegetable soup, Bemy moved in. It was Clare's dream to open a restaurant. Sick of their part-time jobs, they begged and borrowed enough to rent the meat market, but came up short when time came to pay the friends of friends who designed and built the kitchen. In the end, they took in five male partners.

Yes, Clare and Bemy, in their haste and youth, made five mistakes: Frank, the genius physicist who built a giant telescope and wore holey overalls without underwear; Ron, the son of a wealthy minister, who joined the communal endeavor for revolutionary purposes and called the vegetarian restaurant a true food conspiracy; Ozzie, who sang Italian love songs as he kayaked to work in a bright pink sweater; Michael, who rode his bicycle across America and loaned Clare and Bemy a thousand dollars after they gave him a place to stay; finally, LB, a self-proclaimed Zen Buddhist and college drop-out who refused to speak at meetings.

Clare and Bemy saw the Monday meetings as war, two against five. Even so, the seven managed to cook together, pay bills and joke with the customers the other six days of the week. Bemy thought she would discover the heart of America running a successful restaurant, but she found the heart was cold, reptilian. Clare was about to turn twenty-one, graduate from college and move with her boyfriend to New York City. Bemy, two years younger, hadn't yet figured out her next move.

Bemy rinsed her mouth, splashed her face with water and finger combed her hair. Facing the inevitable in the bathroom mirror, she felt trapped waking up to LB. His every look confirmed that once you sleep with a man he thinks he owns your body forever. What she and Clare needed to get out of there was nothing less than a Trojan Horse.

Tying a clean white cotton apron around her like body armor, Bemy crossed Soup a la Victorine off the day's menu and scribbled in her favorite tomato saffron soup. But tension in the kitchen was thick: at the far counter, LB pushed the weight of his taught body into the dough. He hated the dough. He loved the dough. Over and over he folded and punched until satisfied, then he set it in a bowl to rise. After washing his hands, he shook the water all over the kitchen rather than drying them on a towel, and climbed the stairs to the storage loft overhead.

Bemy yanked open the metal handle on the walk-in cooler to gather soup ingredients: two crates of tomatoes, five big white onions, a bunch of parsley and the bag of vegetable scraps for stock. She eyed the wood sorrel they picked in the Black Hills: what a beautiful night it was, driving out past the field with the appaloosa, beneath the freeway and south of the one-room schoolhouse, the dirt roads twisting through the hills toward the Pacific, deep into the rainforest. The stars were so close they made her lonely. She fell asleep in the back of the truck on the way home and woke with a jolt, remembering that she forgot to let Ruth know she'd be home late. The last two days, the oil tank at their rental house was empty and yesterday they boiled water and shared a bath.   Ruth snapped photos of Bemy emerging through steam from the open bathroom door, her torso white like a birch, her arms above her head and fingers dangling like branches and twigs.

"Did your roommate throw you out?" LB asked. He half turned from the dough, slicing it into loaves.

"I didn't think you talked, LB. I mean, you haven't talked at our Monday meetings in three years, even to answer a direct question. Since you asked, Frank forgot to drop me off last night after going to the Black Hills and I didn't want to walk home. Ted Bundy tried to lure a woman at the college into his white van last week with a fake cast."

"Afraid?"

"Just not ready to die. Are you?"

With no answer forthcoming, she concentrated on slicing onions into perfectly thin membranes. Sautéed in butter, the onions melted into the soup, creating a slight texture and a mild bite to the tongue, just enough to make the soup interesting. She tried to remember what had attracted her to LB three years ago as she reached past him for the clipboard of scribbled recipes: onions, leeks, minced peeled and seeded tomatoes, parsley, bay leaf, thyme and salt. That was it—basil, lots of garlic, black pepper, two cups of uncooked rice and ten cups of stock.

LB set the loaf pans on the six-burner stove top for the second rise. Good, he was almost done, she thought. Backing off as he struck a match to light the oven, he lingered, holding the burning match in front of her. She guessed he wanted her to find the flame profound.

"Go ahead and light the fucking oven, LB," she said.

His brown eyes drilled into her. She shivered. She had no empathy for him. She didn't like herself around him. He scrubbed his hands in cold water, scraping with his fingernail at the dried pieces of dough, his fists red like potatoes. He shook the water off and patted his face, pulled his ponytail, snorted, and retied the red string belting his jeans. Finally, finally, he again ascended the stairs to the loft.

What a relief to be alone, she thought. It was crazy how he psyched her out. Crushing basil and thyme with the glass mortar and pestle, she decided that solitude is what to get up for at this hour. Half wakefulness, a mild sweet fragrance of herbs, a sip of tea—just one hour of privacy and she'd be able to cope. The cooling tomatoes stung like jellyfish as she removed the peels and cut the core for compost. Steam mushroomed as she stirred the tomatoes into the pan of sautéed parsley, leek and onion. Pouring the stock through a sieve, she set the soup to simmer and gently crushed the crimson threads of saffron between her fingers.

LB stood in the middle of the kitchen, again, this time biting his knuckle. A vein in his neck bulged as he searched her eyes. Waiting for him to speak, she admitted that she had developed a bad habit of letting men pick her rather than the other way around.

"What now?" Bemy said.

"The anaconda is loose."

"What anaconda?"

"It's gone. The lock on its cage is broken. It could be anywhere."

"The Dickens' snake?" she said. Wiping her juicy hands on her apron, she nervously scanned the floor. "What's a snake doing in the restaurant?"

LB's voice was barely audible. "Last night after we closed I brought the snakes down. My house was too cold–no central heating–and when I came in this morning the anaconda was gone. I figured–it's got to be in the loft or the rafters above the dining room."

"You mean you moved the snakes into the loft without consulting the rest of us?"

"Like I said, it was too cold at the house."

"But it doesn't make sense to bring snakes into a restaurant. Right now, that snake could be in the kitchen or the Odd Fellows Hall upstairs or at the printers next door. Why the hell didn't you tell me earlier? LB, we've got to find it! We can't open for lunch with a snake on the loose."

Bemy grabbed a round-nose vegetable knife and followed LB up the stairs to the loft. The single light bulb was dim. Her eyes widened but she couldn't make anything out. He thrust a flashlight at her and began methodically going through the contents of boxes: dishes, extra bread pans, toilet paper, clothes, three years of dead blenders. Goosebumps rose on her arms. Last night she came up to the loft to get the sleeping bag and didn't notice the glass cages. Now she saw the empty one, its lid off to one side, the lock broken.

"A snake can mangle metal like that?" Bemy said. She shined the light on two very big snakes slithering together in another glass case. Are they mating, she wondered, or just refolding? Maybe they are getting ready to break loose like the anaconda. Then she noticed a third cage filled with squirming white mice. "God damn you," she whispered.

A silent mantra focused her brain: LB is creepy,

sneaky, stinky. She and Clare had thought this for a long time. The three of them briefly lived together one summer and Bemy and Clare had it out with him on a Thanksgiving retreat: all seven partners hiked a fresh killed turkey twelve miles through the Olympic rainforest to a deserted hunting lodge with a functioning wood stove and no electricity. It was LB who had arranged the sleeping bags in one of the upstairs rooms before darkness fell. After the feast, Clare and Bemy went up to bed. They found their sleeping bags on opposite sides of the room and moved them next to each other. LB snuck up stairs and shined the flashlight back and forth in their faces. They screamed and Frank ran up from the wood stove below and took LB away. Clare wanted to leave right then but Bemy talked her out of it. They never would have made it across the Hoh River in the dark.

After the retreat, the guys agreed to sell the restaurant. They placed an ad in *Mother Earth News*, and the Dickens, a couple from the Midwest, offered to buy it. They drove across the country and moved into LB's house. But now Frank and some of the others had changed their minds about selling. Ron accused "the girls" of destroying something beautiful. Discussions about selling ended in arguments. Each week, Clare and Bemy had to start with a fresh appeal: they brought up names of prospective new partners who might want to buy-in; ways to expand the menu; a take-out pizza every night, not just Saturday. All the while, they had to deal with Ron's little quips and Frank's defense of LB's disgruntled silence.

"It's in here," LB said. He took the flashlight from her and shined through a small opening in a concrete wall left open for ventilation: all they could see were rows of rafters above the dining room ceiling.

"Can it kill us?" she asked. "I mean, which is it with the anaconda– poison or strangulation?"

"Strangulation, but not without reason. Just pretend you're the animal you are and listen for the snake."

Bemy felt for the knife, wishing it was a meat cleaver. The anaconda will wrap around the Governor's wife's ankle during lunch rush and the city will close us down, she thought. Or *The Morning Star* headline will read: GIRL STRANGLED BY SNAKE IN RESTAURANT LOFT. No, LB isn't getting rid of me this way, she told herself. A snake is not a good ending to this three-year venture.

Hovering at the opening in the concrete wall, tears surfaced. But the thought of telling Clare the snake story burned through the butterflies in her belly. She wasn't going to get screwed by LB or the snake. A woman at last month's consciousness raising meeting had argued that the snake wasn't evil, it freed Eve. Eden was walled. Think about it, she said. Knowledge is a good thing. We have to read stories from a woman's point of view.

"After you," Bemy said.

LB searched the rafters with the flashlight before

struggling through the small opening, inching forward, hands and knees stretching between the rafters. Before he was out of reach, he passed her the flashlight.

"Stay on the two-by-fours," he warned. "The other is only sheetrock. You'll land in the dining room if you step on it."

Bemy imagined that the Cleopatra-like snake glowed in the dark. She looked for something beautiful as she climbed through the hole. Her muscles quivered as her nostrils filled with dust. Pulling her leg through, she lost her balance and stabbed the aluminum duct above her head with the knife. BOOM! The sheetrock gently cracked as she landed on it. Scrambling back onto the rafters, she realized she needed both hands to hold on, and ditched the flashlight and knife.

"Where are you?" she said.

"Over here." LB was surprisingly close.

It was like crawling through graves long eaten, only the rectangular spaces of coffins remaining. Hundreds of gritty dust snakes hung from the joists above, like decaying skins shed long ago. They caught in her hair and dragged across her neck. A snake after-place. Isn't a snake's body all muscle, she wondered? And if we don't kill it, how will we woo it back into its cage?

LB lit a match and held it high and low as he scooted along the rafter in a squatting position toward the far wall. His head was illuminated in a halo. When the match died, Bemy held onto a single rafter on all fours without breathing. When the next light flickered between his fingers, she leaped from joist to joist. Crouched next to him, both of their shadows loomed and swayed against the crawl space walls. His forehead was beaded with sweat. The smell of his burning flesh reminded her of their first meeting; she wanted to please him; she wanted at least a word or a smile from him: she wanted to know her body and its limitations.

"Where?" she whispered.

He fumbled in his pocket for the book of matches and lit yet another. Moving the flame to the right and left along the next rafter, she saw nothing except dirty sheet rock and a shadow. But that was it. The snake stretched dark and mottled alongside the wooden rafter.

LB inhaled and exhaled slowly.

"It had to take a shit," he said. LB grinned, pleased that snakes and humans shared this biological function. The snake's breakout made sense.

Bemy sniffed the faint dusty stench. The shiny pile of excrement was just beyond the dagger of sunlight now coming in through the fan blades in the wall. The sun was up. It was springtime. Birds squabbled over a nest outside the building and someone shouted on the sidewalk. The piano in the dining room burst with a Mozart sonata: Josh, the messy, rude, homeless teenager they fed in trade for dishwashing had arrived for breakfast. Bemy scampered back across the rafters toward the kitchen as fast as she could.

"I'm calling the ASPCA," she said.

"No don't!" he said, gritting his teeth. "I got it."

After crawling back through the hole in the concrete wall, she turned to watch. LB carried the anaconda out in front of him, a hand at either end of the snake stretched like a tight-rope walker's baton. Crouched and barefoot, he moved toward her in a squatting position, his powerful toes grasping the rafters with agility. He whispered hoarsely: "Push the cage next to the wall and get the lid ready."

Bemy was there for him. A duo, one last time. Not sex, but LB's partner in a strange breathless stunt, nonetheless. It was then that her very first glimpse of him came to her: he was meditating in the shaggy front yard of a communal student house, the sun shining on the soles of his bare feet.

LB reached through the concrete hole, tail first and coiled the snake into the glass box. She slammed the lid down while LB crawled through the concrete wall. She left him sitting on top of the cage like Rodin's *Thinker.* Downstairs, she removed her apron and sweater, washed her face and hands, brushed the webs of dust from her hair. Studying herself in the mirror, she whispered: if you ever fall in love, if there is such a thing, it will be with someone skilled at using words.

OVERLOOK MOUNTAIN

JULIA, Lolo and the twins lived at Old Red, a communal house just outside of Woodstock with eight children, three mothers, two fathers and miscellaneous other adults during the 1990s. Stevie was the oldest kid. Next was Lolo, two years younger. The others were babies or toddlers, like the twins. Because there were three mothers, the children called them by their first name. When Lolo was twelve, she moved with Julia and the twins to John's house in town. John, the twins' father, moved to California a few months after, and Lolo took up the bulk of the childcare. She picked the twins up at kindergarten, cooked pasta or rice and a steamed vegetable, bathed them, brushed their teeth and read *Charlotte's Web* aloud four nights a week while Julia's jazz trio performed at local clubs. Lolo babysat while Julia worked odd shifts at the health food store stocking shelves; during the Saturday morning meditation class she taught in their living room; and Sunday afternoons when Julia's three long-time students arrived, one after the other, for piano lessons.

"Ma," Lolo said. "Did you get time off at Sunflower so we can do the birthday hike? Carol offered to babysit."

Hearing Lolo call her "Ma," like the twins, made Julia tender. She regretted how fast time passed at Old Red. She thought moving into town would stop the whirlwind. Instead, it enabled her to work more hours. Mother and daughter danced delicately around issues of freedom and responsibility: Lolo rose to every occasion so Julia supported Lolo's independence, with the exception of her dropping out of school to study for the GED last spring and even then, Julia did not say no.

New signs were posted along the mile and a half hike to the top of Overlook Mountain: *Beware of Rattlesnakes; Stay on the trail.* The trail was so steep that stepping off in most places meant falling off a cliff. Loose rocks of various sizes made the switchbacks tricky, even when the ground was dry. The way down was always treacherous. Last birthday, Lolo wore sneakers and lost both of her big toe nails, which took six months to grow back.

Where the trail flattened near the top, they passed the ruins of a 1920's lodge that burned. All that remained was concrete and stone. From there, Lolo and Julia headed over to the metal fire tower. Four new wooden picnic tables had been installed since last year.

They set their backpacks at the only empty table and took turns swigging from the water bottle.

"Let's climb the tower before lunch," Julia said.

The thin handrail and narrow steps always felt rickety. Like a game, they paused at each of the nine landings to take in the widening view of the Hudson River valley, stretching north and south. To the west, three lakes nestled in the Catskills. At the top, looking eastward, the Berkshire peaks in Massachusetts sat in a cloud. Lolo and Julia breathed in the cool clean air before heading down. Across from each other at the picnic table they watched squirrels chase each other up and down the trees and birds peck in the dusty earth. Three college age boys speaking Chinese sat down at the other end of their table as they unpacked their lunch of leftover Greek salad and cold pizza. A stranger made the rounds from table to table, offering hikers a treat from his paper bag. As he approached, he smiled into each person's eyes.

"Thanks," said one of the boys. He turned to his friends: "It's pineapple."

"Mine's apricot," said another.

Julia pulled a fig from the bag, smiled, and took a bite. Lolo declined the fruit, but offered the man a chocolate cupcake with frosting that Julia baked. He lifted his hat off his shaven head. His eyes crinkled into a smile like sardines. A loose brown shirt, pants of the same woven material, and sandals signaled to Lolo that he came from far away. He bowed and returned to the log where he left a small backpack. Lolo watched him pull the wrapper off the cupcake and take a bite.

"I'm fifteen today, Julia," Lolo said. "I can keep a secret. Tell me who my father is."

"Happy Birthday, Lolo," Julia said. "If I could give you any gift, it would be the art of slowing time."

"Last week a guy playing guitar on the village green claimed to be my biological father. I told him, no way! Julia had a virgin birth."

Julia laughed. "Imagine how Mary felt with people broadcasting the story of her birth in the manger."

"Right," said Lolo. "And tight-lipped Joseph standing by as if he didn't know the truth." She took a bite of the cupcake. It was Julia's mother's WWII recipe, made with oil rather than butter. The sour milk, baking soda and cocoa gave it a tangy dark chocolate flavor. After a second bite, Lolo handed the cupcake to Julia. "How many men did you sleep with when you were trying to get pregnant with me? I mean, can you give me a list of names so I can cross them off when they try to claim me? I prefer a scientific approach over a surprise."

Julia licked her fingers and took a swig of water. "I had something called endometriosis. It's a thickening of the lining of the uterus that makes conceiving difficult. It took over three years, so I'm afraid I asked more than I intended. Sometimes strange men tell ME that you are their daughter."

"Yikes," sighed Lolo. "But if they were my father, wouldn't they have to pay child support?"

"I never wanted that."

"Not even from my sperm donor? I mean, my father?"

"It wasn't like that with your father, Lolo. We fell in love. We weren't trying to conceive."

"So my birth is really a tragedy because you couldn't live together?"

Julia smiled. The boys at the table were packing up. She waited until they headed back down the trail before continuing. "Love is never a tragedy."

Lolo pouted, exactly as she had as a three-year-old. "So tell me. I want to know."

"Your father is dead."

The lie smacked mother and daughter. It put an end to Lolo's needling of Julia. There was nothing romantic about having a sperm donor for a father or even being a love child, as Julia referred to her. She didn't think the freedom to have sex with whomever should be called love. But the news that she was a *real love child*. This was a nugget she would savor forever.

————

Stevie tapped Lolo's bedroom window, calling her name. His voice caught in the lullaby of the Millstream that flowed behind the house. She remembered the lock clicking on Julia's bedroom door around one-thirty, followed by sounds of sex. She laid awake, wondering if Julia brought home someone new.

"Lolo!" Stevie pleaded.

This time she jumped up. Already dressed in sweatpants, socks and a flannel shirt, she grabbed her coat and tip-toed down the hall. Squeezing through the broken sliding door in the living room, she stepped into her rubber boots on the screened porch. Stevie's old pick-up was parked at the corner, the back-end filled with the usual metal scraps and welding equipment. Lolo kissed Carol's cheek as she slid into the cab next to her and buckled her seatbelt. The points of the moon twisted in tree branches as Stevie downshifted on the switchbacks of Ohayo Mountain road. By starlight, Lolo made out the prayer flags strung across house porches and the gold domes of the Tibetan Monastery pressed against Overlook Mountain. Where the road took a steep downhill turn, Stevie screeched on the breaks and pulled over at Magic Meadow.

"Give me some words," Carol called.

"Terrific," Lolo shouted. "Radiant. Humble."

Carol sprayed foam across a rock outcropping, writing sideways to graffiti the letters. The can empty, she touched a lighter to the foam and the three jumped back: an incandescent green flame rolled like the Aurora Borealis off the rock until, its fuel spent, they stood in darkness. A curve of moon lifted above the woods like a winking smiley face, the red planet as its one eye. Their laughter in the meadow sounded like a snarl of coyotes in an eating frenzy.

Next, Stevie shined the truck's headlights across Magic Meadow and set up a large metal ring welded on a stand. He piled heavy rocks on top of the stand and further secured it by twisting wire around the ring and pulling it taught between trees on either side. Lolo and Carol dragged a mattress from the truck and placed it on the downhill slope, just beyond the ring. Stevie fetched two buckets of pond water and set them nearby as a precaution. Finally, he screwed his camera to the tripod, moved it back far enough to take in the whole scene and adjusted its legs for stability.

"So what's it going to be?" Carol asked.

"Put this on." He tossed them each a flame retardant coverall and stepped into a pair of his own, shoes and all. "Tie the hood close to your face. Tuck your hair inside."

Stevie was known at school for his Friday night festooning and welcomed the kids that gathered at the edge of the woods. He learned to juggle oranges when he was ten and by eleven, he rode around town on a unicycle. In eighth grade, he won first place at the school science fair for an exhibit demonstrating how humans learned to resist gravity and walk upright.

"Rolling," he said, and lit the hoop. A thin ring of orange flame blossomed. His knees bent, he pushed off the ground and dove through the hoop. Somersaulting, he landed on his feet, raised his arms to Lolo and Carol, and bowed. Claps smarted from neighborhood kids watching at the roadside.

Carol jumped on the balls of her feet, flailed her arms and then focused. Her left foot hit the ring as she jumped and belly flopped onto the mattress. Flames frolicked as the hoop swung back and forth. Flush with adrenalin, she hooted.

Lolo swiped her fingers through the flame and feeling no pain, tucked her head. Like a bullet, she shot through the hoop and rolled into the dewy darkness. Knowing the flame's short life, she jumped back in line, rubbing a bruised shoulder. After her second jump, only the truck's ghostly headlights illuminated Magic Meadow.

"I want to watch Philippe Petit practice tightrope walking," said Lolo.

"How about Friday," said Carol. "My morning classes are canceled."

"If it's not raining," said Stevie. "He practices for three hours, so it's a big commitment."

Stevie loaned Lolo *The Thinking Body*, a book Petit suggested he read when the two met at the row of mailboxes at the end of their street. "Actors need to learn how to bring movement into consciousness to control their body and make adjustments," Petit said.

Soon after, they had a plan. Lolo cleared brush. Carol spread a blanket and set out a bottle of water. They laid on their stomachs in their winter coats half an hour before Petit appeared. As he climbed a ladder to the barn's flat roof, Stevie lifted binoculars to his eyes. Petit turned his fifty-pound pole perpendicular to the wire and stepped out. He walked the length between the two barns on the quarter-inch wire, turned and walked back. Then he did it again. And back and forth again. Lolo realized that a commitment to practicing was the only way to be good at something.

The three friends watched the video of Petit's 1974 walk between the World Trade Towers many times at Lolo's house while they babysat the twins. His team snuck eight tons of equipment to the top of the towers. The week he walked eight times back and forth, Petit had stepped on a nail but proceeded as planned anyway. As he talked to the gulls and the cops waiting to arrest him, Lolo imagined Charlotte secretly knitting a web of silk with her spinnerets to catch him in case he fell, as he had once during practice, luckily breaking only a few ribs. Now, as Petit sat in the middle of the wire he stretched his legs out in front and laid flat. For the trio of friends watching from the woods, it wasn't at all like pulling the curtain back and seeing Oz as a human being: it was seeing Petit as God.

The sky was blue, unclouded in every direction, and the temperature sixty-eight degrees the day Stevie, Carol and Lolo drove to the Trailways Bus Station in Kingston. From there it was a two-hour bus ride into New York City. Lolo watched Stevie and Carol from across the aisle, curled together in sleep like the twins. She breathed with them as their bodies rose and fell in unison. She wondered if they had sex on her living room couch on Friday nights when he slept over. Lolo always went to bed first, before Carol walked home, and Julia was never back from her gig before one a.m. Several times a week Stevie picked Carol up from her private school in Poughkeepsie. Maybe they went to Stevie's house or maybe they parked at some dead-end along the Hudson. Lolo looked out the window at the passing landscape and wrote in her notebook: I want to have a thinking body like Petit; write and perform like Shakespeare; love as Stevie loves; be compassionate as Carol; spin silk strong as iron, like Charlotte; flap my wings like Mick and Mia.

At the Forty-Second Street bus terminal, they boarded the downtown E train to Cortlandt Street and walked to the World Trade Center Plaza. Men and women on their lunch hour hurried past. A tour group paused, as their leader waved a small orange flag. Altogether, the group pointed upward at the towers and clicked their cameras. A wind tossed Lolo's hair across her face. Scrunching her hands in her pockets, she found an empty bench and laid down. That was the plan: to focus on the sky where Petit walked. He forced himself to look down at the plaza so he'd have a memory of it. That gave Lolo courage. She had to prepare Julia for her departure. It was happening—improbably, unstoppably —like Charlotte's egg sack ballooning; like a man walking a tightrope 1,368 feet above New York City.

———

The Woodstock town green was a place of vitality, like the old reptilian brain: a place for sleeping, eating, drinking, smooching, or just breathing. Stevie, Carol and Lolo considered it their homestretch. It's where Stevie saw his mother kiss his sixth-grade teacher; where he learned to swear; and where, one dark night, he dislocated his hip wrestling two guys from New York City. For Carol, the town green was the place where she staged her plays and collected money for the women's shelter; the place she drank coffee and sometimes harder stuff. For Lolo, it was her lookout: she searched for a man, tall as she was tall, with broad cheekbones and her signature teardrop nostrils.

On weekends, Lolo painted her face with tiny flowers and wore an old white sailor top with the square collar and white bell bottom pants. She scanned the passersby, jotting observations in a notebook. Not only was it men who approached Lolo with her family history, various women, some she knew as mothers of her classmates, whispered the minutiae of her birth. She piled their words like sticks and stones to puzzle together. Even as their details didn't add up, these tales made Lolo feel like she was part of the big bang, a speck of gold in the expanding universe.

It was during Carol's production of *King LEAR in Fourteen Words* that Lolo first felt the presence of a father. Flyers posted around town might lure him to the performance, she thought. Townspeople kept their eye out for her, offering her rides when they passed her walking the twins to and from kindergarten, violin lessons and birthday parties in the snow and rain.

Stevie blew a trumpet and drivers on Tinker Street slowed, their necks hanging out their windows as they passed the green. He wore a gold cardboard crown with LEAR stenciled in black. His three daughters wore their names on their foreheads: Carol cast herself as GONERIL; a boy named Django played REGAN; and Lolo was CORDELIA.

"How much do you love me?" LEAR asked his three daughters.

GONERIL and REGAN raised large placards with a hundred hearts drawn in red marker while CORDELIA lifted her sailor top to reveal a T-shirt painted with one anatomically correct human heart. Swayed by GONERIL and REGAN's abundance, LEAR kicked CORDELIA off the green.

"No Father!" CORDELIA cried. Her voice carried like a loon in the night, ghostly and sonorous, startling the audience.

LEAR turned to GONERIL and REGAN. *"Take my castle."*

His two oldest daughters smiled. But when LEAR's back was turned, GONERIL and REGAN kicked him off the green, just as he had CORDELIA.

"I'll save you," CORDELIA cried. She ran back toward LEAR, but it was too late. GONERIL poured

pretend drops of poison from a paper cup down REGAN's throat. She then stabbed herself with a sharp point of a cardboard knife. LEAR staggered back onto the green to find his three daughters prostrate on the ground. He laid beside them and raised a placard with a broken heart.

As the audience clapped, the actors passed their hats. Django walked around, strumming his guitar, calling out: *The tricks of patriarchy may stem from a seemingly harmless question but as Shakespeare demonstrates in King Lear, the play ends in tragedy.* Lolo's collection of coins jingled in her pockets as she crossed Tinker Street to the benches outside the ice cream store where people ate their cones. A man sitting tall, stood as she approached. She smiled inwardly at the stranger from Overlook Mountain who passed the paper bag of dried fruit. Eye to eye, he bowed his head and they parted in silence.

Stevie, Carol and Lolo made grilled cheese sandwiches at Julia's and when Mick and Mia went down for a nap, the three friends assessed the performance. Carol announced that they brought in more than any other play—seventy-six dollars and forty-three cents. Stevie said that they needed a second camera and tripod to make a better video. Lolo stood and twirled around to face her best friends, who waited expectedly. She hesitated.

"Here is what I have to say about the performance," Lolo began. "Shakespeare wrote King Lear four hundred years ago. Carol wrote her version in fourteen words. Two of those words sum up my life. When I yelled out my line—*No, father*—I didn't include the comma. Essentially, I announced to the village that I have no father. This action has freed me. The search for my father is over."

RED MILLENNIUM

CAM RANG the cash register all afternoon at the Five & Ten, one town over from her own in upstate New York. It was New Year's Eve and nearly everyone who stopped in to buy party hats and horn blowers knew Cam. Not only was she a beauty, she was the rare seventeen-year-old with a savvy upbeat attitude and she was saving for college. In the fall she would embark on her dream of becoming a shrink, a dream she held since she was seven, since her mother's boyfriend Rollie came into her life and she began seeing Mrs. V., her therapist. Going to college meant moving away from her complicated family, to Westchester, a suburb of New York City. This was the journey her mother had taken twenty years earlier, but Cam was resolved not to make her mother's mistakes.

Light snow turned to mist around three o'clock and Main Street took on a wet black sheen. Cam was relieved that snow would not dampen the big millennium celebration at the Danceteria, nor slow Rollie's drive home from the Hamptons where he and his new wife, Tina, were looking to buy a fixer-upper. Like their wedding, the millennium would be a night Cam would remember. Tina helped her shop online for her slinky red dress and when it arrived, Cam danced like a firecracker through the house.

"Holy shit," said Rollie.

"Totally downtown," said Tina.

At four-thirty, Cam guessed that her girlfriends were already primping in front of the mirror. She couldn't bear working at the store another half hour! Cam wanted to relax in a warm bubble bath, hook the string of pearls around her neck and dab perfume behind her ears—Christmas gifts from Rollie and Tina. While straightening the cosmetic rack, she discovered a red lipstick she hadn't seen before and rang it up on the cash register. If only her boss would emerge from the back office and hurry Cam home to dress, but she was a realist.

"It's foolish to expect computer and electrical crashes at the stroke of midnight," her boss said. "The hoarding of canned food and bottled water will just artificially drive up the GNP."

Rollie laughed when Cam told him this. "Your boss might think differently if there was a run on items at the Five & Ten."

The shiny white mustang Rollie rebuilt pulled up in

front of the store and the black box in Cam's head labeled "Mother" popped open. Giddy and blubbering, her mother hopped out and disappeared into the liquor store next door. Cam concentrated on the boy slumped in the passenger seat, a baseball cap pulled down over his face. It was probably Bobby who sat next to her in math, or Jay in her English class. Unfortunately, she and all her friends would know who scored with her mother as soon as the boy started bragging. It had been four years since Cam's mother let her garden go to seed; four years without a mother-daughter connection, even if she was still Cam's legal guardian. Their last contact was the angry word "No" her mother scrawled across Cam's five-page plea for financial help when she received an early acceptance to college.

As sometimes happened when she got upset about her mother, the "Father" box popped open. Cam heard again the sound of his US Army issued gun going off. She focused on her father's green diamond shaped eyes, all she really remembered of him. Luckily, Rollie came along and built Cam and her mother a house with wallpapered bedrooms and a swimming pool. He brought music, art and politics to the dinner table. Most startling, and hopeful to Cam, were Rollie's frank discussions of surviving his brutal father, a German Nazi who snuck into the US after World War II. The way Cam saw it, Rollie's mother saved him from becoming his father, and Rollie saved her from becoming her mother.

But Cam and Rollie were both shell-shocked when, just last year, the extended family detailed the not so rosy picture of her mother's childhood. The fact also surfaced that Cam's father killed himself after he happened to stop home on his lunch hour to find his co-worker in bed with her mother. It took Rollie and Mrs. V. months to get Cam beyond that swift water.

At five o'clock, Cam's boss found her staring out the window at the car. She placed her hand in Cam's and gently squeezed. When its wheels squealed away from the curb, Cam conjured all her brain power to lock "Mother" back in the imaginary box and wish her boss Happy New Year.

Inhaling the damp night air revived Cam's young spirit. Walking around the corner to her parked car, she imagined the softness of her fiery red dress as she danced. Last night when Rollie called, she told him that her wicked mother had done an extraordinary deed bringing him into her life: he was the best father a girl could ever want, and the only parent she had.

Alanis Morissette blasted on the radio as Cam shifted into reverse and backed out of the dark parking lot. A lone car looped through the hills behind her, past lit farmhouses and dark majestic barns. A mile from home her headlights caught the white tail of a deer flick danger! Danger! Would it turn and flee, or dash across the road? Pushing the accelerator to the floor, Cam honked and swerved to get past the deer and up the hill. But her small car lifted off the road and over her neighbor's cow pasture: she couldn't steer or break. *She had not fastened her seatbelt! She always fastened her seatbelt!* Slapped against the cold dark field, the car door popped and Cam's perfect body swung out into the night. Too early for the Danceteria. Too early for college. Too early for the people of the towns who loved her.

IT'S THE WATER

JOSEY WAS the tallest in her class until senior year of high school when Boone overtook her. She was physically memorable–lanky, with a long nose, long brown hair and a wide mouth. Her passion was large, too, even palpable, as proceeds from an early failed marriage enabled her to take on volunteer projects, one after another. But most difficult for her older sister, Ella, was Josey's gregariousness. She found Josey's storytelling to be over-the-top, embarrassing, even false. Still, Ella was grief-stricken when Josey died of breast cancer. They hadn't seen each other in a year and it set her back, just as their father's sudden death had decades earlier. As the last living family member, Ella cleaned Josey's Seattle apartment, gave away her lovely things and organized a memorial.

"Where the fuck am I?" Ella yelled at the GPS. She pulled over to the side of the two-lane road and got out of the car, dazed by the barren landscape. "Why did you tell me to get off the Highway? I *know* my way to Olympia!"

Ella had driven through the familiar Capitol State Forest only moments before and now found herself tip-toeing through tall, wet grass that grew between large symmetrical eight-foot mounds almost 30-feet wide. Assuming she trespassed on aboriginal burial grounds, she wondered how many skeletons surrounded her. Her good leather boots were soaked, her toes wet. She was hard on herself, seemingly making mistake after mistake, but the sight of a parking lot with half a dozen cars cheered her. A real bathroom made of wood and concrete further lifted her spirits. After using the facility, she washed her face and took a deep breath. Then she saw it: an arrow pointed toward the 15-mile Mima Falls Trail Loop.

Ella gasped, tucked her head and wept.

The GPS had directed her to the very spot of her father's heart attack thirty years earlier. Her mother had heard from an old friend in his walking group that he complained of dizziness and arranged to meet them back at the car. They later found him sitting cross-legged, white bird poop streaking his face. Scanning the sky for predatory birds, Ella felt bad that she never reached out to him. She was nine when her mother stole her and Josey from the house in the middle of the night: they drove to her grandmother's tulip farm outside Aberdeen, which is where Ella still lived.

The GPS reminded Ella that she was on the fastest route to the Universal Unitarian Congregation in Olympia. Not wanting to believe it, Ella considered turning around but instead, pushed her father out of her mind and her foot on the gas. Reaching Interstate 5, she took the downtown Olympia exit and headed up the westside. The GPS guided her down side streets she didn't know existed.

"It's a miracle I made it," she told the Universalist who greeted her.

"Would you like me to place a card on each chair? I'd be happy to do that for you."

"Sure," Ella said. She gave her the stack printed with Josey's headshot and went back to her car for the yellow tulips. The flowers brightened the plain room of wooden walls and windows. As strangers quietly entered and took their seats, she was disappointed that neither Josey's ex-husband, Tom, a local attorney, nor Boone, Josey's first boyfriend, had showed up. Promptly at two o'clock, she stood at the podium between the flowerpots and thanked everyone for coming. Her eyes rolled as she mentioned a few of Josey's escapades, such as the "art" movies she starred in; the lepers she lived with on the Kalaupapa peninsula in Hawaii; and her volunteer work at the local Body Farm where human taphonomy is studied as remains are left exposed to the elements.

Ella invited others to the podium when she finished speaking and retreated to a window ledge at the back of the room. She took out her hearing aids and, like a scold, her father's face floated in front of her. Ella wanted to scream: Why? What did I do wrong? She remembered her mother who leaned on her during the divorce and her hand touched the soft flowing dress she had picked from her mother's closet. She saw her mother and Gabriella sway through the old farmhouse to Frank Sinatra's crooning on the radio. Her mother would have been pleased with the turn-out for Josey.

"Ella, do you remember me?"

Had she fallen asleep? Was the service over? Without hearing aids the world was blurry, even blissful. A world without death. She had seen too many spring flowers cut before full bloom. The need to sell the farm pressed on her. But where would she live? She reinserted her hearing aids, and stood.

"Boone, is that you?"

"I'm glad you recognize me after so many decades." He kissed her forehead gently. That was all she ever wanted from her father. A soft kiss on the forehead.

"How could I forget you? You were practically my brother during high school."

Boone and Josey had always looked more like siblings than she and Josey. He was the same—tall, lean and sun beaten—only gray now. She could still see Josey and Boone racing their bikes between the dry tulip beds of summer, Josey overtaking him every time. More than once she came upon them naked and entwined under a tree. Later, when he bought a motorcycle, they roared off together and disappeared down the road. Josey never lived at home after that, and Ella never forgave her. First she nursed her mother. Then, as if breast cancer was catching, her grandmother. Ella later suffered her own bout of it and Gabriella nursed her through the chemotherapy, which left her hearing impaired; her feet riddled with neuropathy.

"I loved Josey's nose best of all," Boone said. "Like a ballet dancer lifting her slipper to her forehead. It was the way she owned it. Teasing her only forced her head higher."

"Excuse me," said a petite woman dressed in overalls. "I'm Linda, Josey's friend. She gave me this letter a few months ago when she resigned as a volunteer at The Body Farm."

"Hi," Ella said. "Thanks."

"Josey picked a place under a spreading maple," Linda said. "She applied to be interned on the farm and we would like to make that happen."

"I wish I knew," Ella said. "Would it be possible to sprinkle her ashes under the tree?"

Linda shook her head in disappointment. "I'm sorry. We're conducting a scientific study."

Ella grimaced as the guests disappeared through the door. The last was a meticulously dressed man in a black suit who turned and waved his cane. It was Tom, Josey's ex-husband, bearded and bald-headed! She thought for a moment of walking him to his car, but couldn't imagine what to say. Sending him a thank-you note would suffice, she decided.

The Unitarian woman pressed a small stack of leftover cards into Ella's hands, which she tucked in her purse and slung over her shoulder. Like the cards, the tulips looked worn after the event. Boone carried the flowers to the trunk of Ella's car. She elbowed him and pointed to a box.

"Maybe you could help me figure out what to do with Josey's ashes."

"Let me cook you dinner," he said. "I'm the groundskeeper at the old Olympia Brewery on Black Lake. It's a museum now."

Ella hesitated.

"Grilled shrimp tossed with homemade pasta. How does that sound?"

"That's sweet, Boone. I have a few errands. Is six o'clock okay?"

"I'll text the address."

She laughed. "Don't be surprised if my GPS pulls a fast one on me and I get lost."

Boone pointed to the red neon sign visible across the lake: *It's the Water.* "Remember that tagline? Go through the gate and just follow the road."

As promised, she found him standing over the grill in a white chef's apron where the road dead-ended. Retrieving the grilled items with tongs, he walked Ella up the brick steps to his apartment. A sculptural polished copper tank leftover from the brewery divided his kitchen and living room. Logs burned in an arched brick fireplace. The table, set with stoneware and cloth napkins, overlooked Black Lake, ringed with lights like her grandmother's diamond necklace.

Ella sipped a glass of white wine, something she usually declined. She enjoyed Boone's easy smiles and whimsical tales of the fox and the old grey woodchuck, so feisty he backed into his hole beneath the woodshed. After the meal, they sat on the long couch in front of the fire, facing each other, their legs side by side. Boone pulled a blanket from the back of the couch and tucked it over them. Threads of light reflected off the lake and danced across the walls.

She wiggled her toes. "Boone, would you mind giving me a foot massage?"

"Love to," he said. Ella reminded him of Josey just then. He appreciated women who let their wishes be known. Retrieving a bottle from another room, he rubbed rose scented oil into his callused hands and anointed her feet. Her neck relaxed against the arm of the couch, her eyes closed. She felt safe deep in the castle-like brewery. Spooked by neither the mima mounds nor her father's face, she followed his slow kinesthetic movements: he pulled each toe; pressed the space between and the fleshy pads; thumbed her arch; fingered her Achilles heel with one hand while holding it in the palm of his other, and massaged her calf before shifting to the second foot.

"Boone, how many years did you and Josey see each

other two nights a week? She told me that you also had a male lover two nights a week during that time."

"Yes. For years. Always. Whenever she was in town. Even during her marriage to Tom. The man she referred to was George. No one like him has come along since then, although I still occasionally date men."

"Did you see Tom today? He's so old!"

"Josey was just a kid when she married him. I was glad he spoke."

"What did he say?" Ella asked.

He gave her a knowing look, and thought for a moment. "He said love doesn't die with flesh. It's a fuel that once lit, burns into infinity."

She laughed. "That's more poetry than I'd expect from him. He was always so dry."

"Mmm," Boone smiled. "Seeing you brings back those spicy Mexican cookies your mother baked."

"Gabriella's cookies. Mother's beloved friend, remember her? I'll bring you some next time I visit. She rents a place down the road with her nieces and nephews and every spring they help with the harvest."

"I remember a beautiful picture of your mother and Gabriella as girls, like tulips in the field."

"That photograph still hangs in the hall."

Ella took a moment, covered her face and choked on a deep guttural sob. She couldn't believe how life had passed her by. She had plenty of lovers in her youth. Where did they all go? Who was going to come to her fucking memorial? Who will give away all her beautiful things?

"Boone," she said, when her crying jag passed. "I got lost driving through the Black Hills and ended up at the mima mounds, the place my father died."

"Mima Mounds Falls Trail," he said. "That's an exceptional hike. Scientists discovered mima mounds on every continent except Antarctica."

"What are they?"

"It's an ecosystem. The mounds are piles of gravel created by generations of gophers burrowing over 500 years. Water collects in the grass between the mounds. That's where fairy shrimp grow. The gophers live on them."

"Give me a break," Ella sniffled. "What are we, gophers? We had shrimp for dinner!"

"These are freshwater shrimp—crawdads or crayfish."

Pulling her legs to the floor, she sat up. "Tell me how Josey died."

"Exactly like she lived, Ella. Half of those people at the memorial were volunteers like her at the women's cancer connection. Josey loved you, Ella. I'm here for you. I promised her I would be."

Ella moved to the window again. The Lake was spread white with moon shadow, except one edge glowing pink with the red signage. A clarity washed over her murky brain: she couldn't believe it—Boone! A gift from Josey! A life-long friend. She decided right then that she would move to Olympia, the town where she attended college. She'd buy a small house with a view of Puget Sound and sell the farm to Gabriella and her family. She'd make it affordable–their rent could go toward a down payment. She'll leave it to them in her will.

"Let's toss Josey's ashes in the lake and plant the yellow tulip bulbs to mark the spot," she said.

Boone's eyes squeezed closed. His arm reached over the back of the couch for Ella and she held his hand in hers. She had never seen a man cry before. He rubbed his face and whispered: "When the drugs kicked in, Josey smiled like The Mona Lisa blasting off into outer space. We got a glimpse of eternity and I fell back to earth. That's how she died, Ella. Holding my hand."

PREVIEW "ANNA MAGDALENA"

Performance artist Anna Magdalena splays her audience open and leaves them begging for more. More life. More freedom. More imagination. By redefining family, history, myth, time and identity, she prompts readers to take action and forge a life of extraordinary beauty.

Anna Magdalena is a contemporary novel about the power of art, love and imagination in its many forms. Reade Bordeaux, a forty-year-old Seattle plumber, married to Sgt. Becky Smith, is smitten with Anna Magdalena, a New York City performance artist retreated to Willapa, a forgotten Victorian town on the Washington coast. With a snap of her fingers, they land in the New York art world with her acquired family: Saxton, her ex-lover; Lulu, his mother; and Lulu's partner, Kermit Fleur, an old master dealer who takes Reade under his wing. Honey Dearborn and her son

Frank, Reade's prickly neighbor in Willapa, drive the story with mischief, mystery and good fortune even after their death. But Sgt. Becky Smith has some tricks of her own. While Anna Magdalena provokes audiences with disappearing acts, vows, secrets, and outrageous art pieces that take place on NYC roof tops and beds, Becky pulls a fast one. The whole family rallies around Reade and he is awed as Anna Magdalena clicks her heels.

———

CHAPTER 1

As the plane banked over New York City, Reade opened the window shade and got his first glimpse of Manhattan. Skyscrapers saluted the dawn in pointed rows of gold. Even the Atlantic Ocean's undulating surface appeared gold-leafed as the plane circled back toward JFK Airport. Below, the Long Island beaches looked so much like Willapa. Reade remembered how, for a whole year, Anna Magdalena rolled out of his reach like a log in the surf every time he tried to kiss her.

The cab stopped in front of a gray, frost-bitten, four-story warehouse on a triangular piece of land, surrounded by a wire fence, woven with dead vines. He couldn't understand a word the driver said. Not wanting to get killed, fearful that he was in the wrong borough, he refused to get out. The driver pointed to his GPS and grabbed Reade by the armpits. Only then did Reade notice a thin copper pipe draping a red cloth like a big red wound above the door, roughly painted with Anna Magdalena's initials. He apologized and pressed an extra twenty into the driver's palm.

The key was hidden in the drainpipe as promised, and opening the metal gray door, grit and cobwebs covered all but a narrow path through desks and cabinets shoved together in piles. A yellow envelope with his name leaned against the rubble. It contained a pictogram of male body parts cut from magazines taped in rows, titled: *What I Love about Reade*. Below this, in her familiar block print, she wrote, "Enter the door marked RESTROOM." And there she was in a sleeping bag, on a green couch, in a green-tiled bathroom, with three toilets, three mirrors, and three sinks. As Reade undressed, he noticed a drawing on the open concrete shower stall. The Empire State Building leaned toward The Statue of Liberty. In a cartoon bubble, it said: "Come on, light my fire." Liberty was drawn like an exhausted Virgin Mary in heavy drapery juggling a book and torch. She said, "I want updating, not a date."

This should have clued Reade to his next discovery. AM's jet-black bumble of hair was buzzed to the kind of cut his father gave him sitting on the kitchen table at age five. Nothing remained but a Tin Tin tuft of fluff over her forehead. As he maneuvered his cold feet into her sleeping bag, he worried. How would he save her if she tried to fly like Pegasus across the Atlantic? Only luck had kept them from drowning in the deadly Japanese current that swept down from the Aleutians along the Washington coast. His feet had landed on a sandbar, and knotting her thick unleashed hair in his fist, they had scrambled to shore. He should have been forewarned, that the black curls of her pubic were shaved, too, and the new sharp angle of her hip alarmed him. In her favor, she still had two small breasts, two dark, almond-shaped eyes, one sea lion nose, ten fingers, and ten toes. Sex was rehabilitating. Therapeutic. Restorative. When they rolled onto their backs, she offered him the secret fact regarding her disappearance.

"It was a certified letter from Honey Dearborn's attorneys. She left me a building in her will. I had to claim it in person. But before telling you, I needed to know if it was real. This is it, Reade. This warehouse is ours."

"Honey must have skyrocketed the value of your art," he said.

"Yeah, but remember," she said. "I was her last link to Frank, her only son. And she was dying of cancer. With Frank gone, she gave everything away."

Reade could hardly believe the strange scenario. It was so farfetched. Frank Dearborn was his eccentric neighbor in Willapa, and they only met his mother, Honey, after Frank died. Now Honey was dead and had left this building to AM. *More implausible*, Reade thought, *was that AM needed him*. There was work to do.

A place to live. A building to renovate. A permanent performance space. AM's gallerist, Vivian Boo, already had a benefactor's ear about funding for the necessary renovations.

After a cold morning shower, Reade found her note taped to the door: Meet at sundown, 115 Central Park West and 72nd Street, apartment 6B. He found his way to the subway, got off at Union Square, and bought a cup of coffee. Sitting beneath a statue of Gandhi, he watched the great swirl of common: the patter of dogs looping around the dog run; NYC Parks Department workers bent in slow tai chi; the creaky tin-man walk of middle-age heroin addicts and their sorry sad eyes; preschoolers, hand-in-hand, dressed in oversized orange t-shirts; tall bronze models walking like jaguars —toe forward, shoulders back, rotating hips with each step—and their neatly unshaved equivalents dressed in business suits with suave, wet-looking hair swooped off their foreheads; shoppers at the green market carrying heavy recyclable bags; high school girls in a fistfight; the bell ringer's cry of *just one penny for the homeless*; lovers entwined like downed trees on the lawn; the steaming sculpture on the building to the south with electronic numbers counting every second; Lee Strasberg's blue banner, limp in the green leafy trees of 15th Street. Every so often, Reade looked for the sky between the buildings to guess how much longer before sunset.

Lulu Rose greeted Reade as he stepped off the elevator on the sixth floor. Her cropped white hair was cut severely, like Anna Magdalena's. Her eyes were painted black, and a flowing white dress emphasized her tan shoulders. Asymmetrical rings of silver clinked on her wrists. Reade selected a glass of sparkling water with lemon when a waiter approached with a tray of drinks. Resting his eyes on the row of Fifth Avenue buildings at the far side of Central Park, his ears tuned to two women sipping red wine on his left.

"Lulu's annual Thanksgiving Day Parade brunch was spectacular," said the tall one with a youthful-looking pixie haircut. The other woman wore bright green hair. Her eyes synchronized with her smile like a puppeteer pulling a string. The first woman continued, "The wind blew the giant Snoopy balloon into the window. We were lucky it didn't break!"

Feeling out of place in cowboy boots still dusty from his farm, a dull sport coat, hair bushy on top and long on his neck, Reade sauntered into the living room. He was taken by an oversized black and white photograph of a birch tree, its ancient curvaceous limbs carved with love notes and initials inside hearts pierced by arrows. Finally, escorted into the dining room, Reade saw Anna Magdalena seated next to Lulu at the head of the table. It was set with white roses, white china, white napkins, white candles, and an enormous amount of silverware, goblets, and wine glasses. He had never seen Anna Magdalena in a dress before and couldn't stop smiling in her direction. Like Lulu, her shoulders were bare. When she turned, he saw her back was also bare to her waist. He was wondering how he'd get through the evening sitting so far from her when the chatter stopped. The guests focused on Lulu, her hands circling over flames of candles. He remembered Anna Magdalena's stick drawings in the Willapa sand, her tales of Shakespeare's bad queens, disobedient wives, daughters in disguise, and stories of powerful women and their erotic likes and dislikes.

"Good evening. Kermit Fleur," said the elderly gentleman to Reade's left. He offered his soft, pale hand.

"Nice to meet you. I'm Reade Bordeaux." Reade lingered on Kermit's thick accent. He felt silly worrying about his own twisted tongue. Born with a speech impediment, Reade never learned to pronounce the letter R properly. His Ma told everyone he was born with a French accent, that is, until she heard the fourth-grade boys taunt him with *Weedy Bodo*.

"Have you seen Caravaggio's *The Denial of Saint Peter* at The Metropolitan Museum of Art? It is a very important picture," Kermit said between spoonfuls of chicken soup. "It was Caravaggio's last painting placed in a museum."

"No. I arrived in New York last night. This is my first visit."

"You must frequent the Metropolitan Museum," Kermit said. He pulled a small leather book from his breast pocket with writing paper and a pen and mapped a tour of his favorite rooms.

"Thank you," Reade said. "I am a friend of Anna Magdalena."

"Yes, I know," he said. "By the way, take a look at the Flemish Masters. Anna Magdalena's face is one they dearly loved. You will find her there. Every picture tells a story."

Waiters patiently bent over each guest with portions of what looked to Reade like his Ma's pot roast, slices of glistening chicken, greens, and noodles. He was beginning to enjoy himself when he noticed a man across the table spying on him through a vase of roses: his one dark pupil appeared between the white petals; his other was covered in a pirate patch. Reade fortified the wall between them with crystal water goblets and empty wine glasses and returned his attention to Kermit's art lecture.

"Neoclassicism was popular at the turn of the nineteenth century. With new engineering methods brought on by the industrial revolution, Greek revival, Gothic and Renaissance architecture appeared in the background of paintings. This was the beginning of modernity."

The one-eyed stranger across the table stood and tipped a bottle of wine toward Reade's glass.

Reade covered it with his hand. "No, thank you. I don't drink."

"Welcome to New York, Reade. And to my childhood home. My name is Saxton. You've met my mother, Lulu? And I see you've met my mother's partner, Kermit."

The two facts Reade recalled from Anna Magdalena's description of her ex-lover practically crushed him on the spot: he wore a pistol in an ankle holster, and he preferred to sleep with strangers of either sex. Reade thought he might be challenged to a duel after dinner. Or worse.

"We worried when Maggie ghosted us," Saxton continued, "but here she is, back to haunt. And, I must add, it's good to have our whore at the table again."

"Whore," Reade said. His tongue was a bouquet of unpreparedness. He turned toward Anna Magdalena, but she wasn't in her seat. Scanning the room, he found her hugging a woman in a pink sari a few chairs away from Lulu. She noticed Reade's face-off with Saxton. The triangle—Anna Magdalena, her lover, and her ex-lover —caused a hushed ripple around the table.

"Call Anna Magdalena an esthetic terrorist, why don't you. Or an angel. Or an artist extraordinaire," Reade said.

"Whore is what I call myself," Saxton said. "Or anyone who makes sex the epicenter of their world. Perhaps virginity is still the aspired state in WILL-A-PA?"

Reade gave Saxton an abrupt nod. He sat down, refusing to engage further. Retrieving his napkin from the floor, he placed it over his lap and turned his attention back to Kermit.

"Mr. Bordeaux, we are breaking the fast. Today is Yom Kippur, the holiest day of the Jewish year. The day we ask both friends and enemies for forgiveness. You are not Jewish, are you?"

"No, I'm not religious."

"As an immigrant in New York, I survived on onion rolls placed on every table at Ratner's," Kermit continued. "Young Jewish immigrants who couldn't speak English like me were given the job of pouring water for customers. In return, we were allowed to eat all the onion rolls we wanted. I learned enough English to join the Army this way. U.S. intelligence needed German speakers. After the war, I started many businesses that failed. Eventually, I opened an exporting business to help Europe rebuild. I exported steel and began to buy impressionist prints and out-of-fashion nineteenth-century religious paintings. That is how I opened my gallery."

Kermit selected two pastel-colored cookies, pink and green, offered by a waiter. Reade selected a yellow cookie that melted into a sweet lemon paste in his mouth. He later learned they were called macarons, a favorite of Anna Magdalena.

"And what is your business?" Kermit asked.

"I'm a plumber by trade," Reade said.

"Oh," Kermit nodded. "That's a useful skill."

But the plain, dull word "plumber" tasted dry and brittle in his mouth so he elaborated. "Humans are driven by the need for fresh water. And like electricity, unless contained, water finds the path of least resistance. Water pipes are necessary yet it's common for them to break in a freeze or an earthquake. Water moves soil, so a broken water pipe can erode a hillside. Great amounts of soil run right over the biggest falls like Niagara and Victoria, sculpting graceful contours of deserts and mountains."

Kermit nodded. He gave Reade his card and untucked his napkin. As he stood, Reade noticed a slight hint of red in Kermit's silver waves of hair. A small plump pillow rested beneath each eye. "Please visit my gallery. I have some pictures I'd like to show you." He patted Reade's shoulder. "Good night, my friend."

Lulu linked Reade's arm and guided him past her friends, nodding and smiling. Anna Magdalena stood in a clutch of guests at the elevator: her stretchy black dress was calf-length; her shoulders now wrapped in petals of woven fabric like a peony. Walking toward her with Lulu, her eyes brightened.

"I hope you enjoyed yourself, Reade," Lulu said.

"I did. Thank you for inviting me. It was so nice to meet you and Kermit and," Reade hesitated, "Saxton."

Lulu paused their stroll. "I wasn't about to give up Maggie when she and Saxton broke up. She's mishpocha —that means family in Yiddish—and now you are mishpocha, too. You have nothing to worry about, Reade. Call me if you need anything."

ABOUT THE AUTHOR

Maureen McNeil is a writer, artist and activist based in Brooklyn and the Hudson Valley. In 2021, her story, *A Strange Breathless Stunt*, was a finalist for the Tiferet Fiction Prize; and *Cooper and Corinna,* won second place for the Barry Lopez Nonfiction Prize. McNeil's first collection, *Red Hook Stories*, was published in 2008; *Dear Red: The Lost Diary of Marilyn Monroe, A Work of Fiction,* in 2017. McNeil lectures on writing, and designs and teaches workshops in partnership with arts and cultural organizations, such as PEN America, The Anne Frank Center USA, Prison Public Memory Project, Yad Vashem, the Morgan Library, the Woodstock Day School and Hudson Area Library.

www.ingramcontent.com/pod-product-compliance
Lightning Source LLC
Chambersburg PA
CBHW071211130626
46555CB00004B/1666